THE
GHOST
OF
WINDY
HILL

The Ghost Of Windy Hill

by Clyde Robert Bulla
illustrated by Don Bolognese

A
LITTLE APPLE
PAPERBACK

SCHOLASTIC INC.
New York Toronto London Auckland Sydney

ISBN 0-590-43286-9

Copyright © 1968 by Clyde Robert Bulla.

All rights reserved. Published by Scholastic Inc.,
730 Broadway, New York, NY 10003,
by arrangement with Thomas Y. Crowell Company, Inc.

APPLE PAPERBACKS is a registered trademark of Scholastic Inc.

12 11 10 9 8 7 6 5 4 3 2 1   1   9/8 0 1 2 3 4/9
Printed in the U.S.A.   11

TO THE McKENZIES
Dorothy and Mac
Carol and Rod

Contents

Evening Visitors   1

Mr. Giddings   8

Windy Hill   13

The Tower   19

At The Crossroads   25

The Man On The Bank   30

A Message From Bruno   35

Miss Miggie   43

The Rag Bag   48

The Crazy Quilt   54

The Room Down The Hall   58

The Sound Of Bells   63

A Strange Story   69

The End Of Summer   76

Evening Visitors

The boy and girl sat on the step in front of the candle shop. They had been waiting for a breeze, but no breeze had come.

Daylight was nearly gone. "We'd better go in," said the boy.

"Let's wait till they call us," said the girl. "It's so hot up in those little rooms."

"It's hot here, too," he said, "and we told them we wouldn't stay out after dark."

"Can't we stay a little longer?" she asked. "Just till the carriage goes by?"

In the distance they could hear the clatter of wheels and horses' hoofs on the cobblestone street.

They waited and watched. The carriage came in sight. It was tall and black, and it moved slowly toward them. A man sat high in the driver's seat. Another man was inside, leaning out the window. He called to them, "You, there!"

The boy stood up. "Yes, sir," he said.

"Does Professor Carver live on this street?" asked the man.

"He lives here," said the boy.

The man looked surprised. "In the candle shop?"

"He rents the rooms over the shop," said the boy.

The carriage stopped. The man got out. "We've found it," he said. "This is the place."

There was a woman in the carriage. "I tell you, we shouldn't have come," she said.

"Of course we should, my dear." The man asked the boy and girl, "Do you know the Professor? Could you take us to him?"

"Yes, sir," said the boy. "Professor Carver is our father."

"Well, well!" said the man. "Would you go and say to him that Mr. Giddings is here?"

The boy and girl ran upstairs. A woman was there in the doorway.

"Mother, it's Mr. Giddings," said the boy.

"He wants to see Father," said the girl.

The woman turned toward the man in the little room behind her. He was sitting under the light, painting a picture. She asked him, "Do you know a Mr. Giddings?"

"I don't think so," said Professor Carver. "No

—wait. Is he short and stout? Does he have small eyes and bushy eyebrows?"

"Yes," said the boy and girl together.

"It's all right," said Professor Carver. "I'll see him."

Mr. Giddings was already on the stairs. He was leading the woman. She tried to draw back. "I'm not going in there!" she said.

"Of course you are, my dear." He led her up to the door. "Good evening," he said. "My name is Giddings, and this is my wife."

"Good evening," said Professor Carver. "This is *my* wife, and these are our children, Jamie and Lorna. Come in."

They all sat down.

"Perhaps you don't remember me," said Mr. Giddings.

"I remember you," said Professor Carver. "You came to the school one day."

"But there was no chance to talk with you there." Mr. Giddings looked at Jamie and Lorna. "What I have to say may seem strange. If you wish to send the children away—"

"I have no secrets from them," said Professor Carver. "Lorna is ten and Jamie is almost twelve. I believe they are old enough to hear whatever you have to say."

"Very well," said Mr. Giddings. "Professor Carver, I first heard of you from my cousin. She comes into Boston every week to study painting in your class. She told me something about you—something I found most interesting."

"Yes?" said Professor Carver.

"She told me," said Mr. Giddings, "that you once lived in a haunted house."

Professor Carver sat straight in his chair.

"Is it true," asked Mr. Giddings, "that you lived in the house and drove out the ghost that was there?"

"How can you ask such a question?" said Professor Carver.

"I was told——" began Mr. Giddings.

"We are not living in the Dark Ages," said Professor Carver. "We are living today, in the Year of Our Lord, 1851!"

"I was told——" Mr. Giddings began again.

"I think I know what you were told," said Professor Carver. "A few years ago I had a friend who believed his house was haunted. I laughed at the idea. He dared me to live in the house for a while. To prove how foolish he was, I moved into the house with my wife and children."

"Your wife and children, too!" said Mr. Giddings.

"Certainly," said Professor Carver. "They are no more afraid of ghosts than I am. We lived there a month. By that time my friend was ready to believe he had no ghost in his house. Is this what you heard?"

"Not quite," said Mr. Giddings. "I was told that you lived in the haunted house and because you weren't afraid, you drove the ghost away."

"Nonsense!" said Professor Carver.

"Some people might not call it nonsense," said Mr. Giddings. "Let me tell you why I came to you."

"I am waiting to hear," said Professor Carver.

"When I was a boy, I lived near a farm called Windy Hill," said Mr. Giddings. "It was the dream of my life to own that farm, even though I was poor and the dream seemed far away. But life was good to me. Last year I was able to buy the farm. My wife and I went there to live. And then——" He turned to his wife. "Tell him, dear."

Mrs. Giddings said in a choked voice, "The house is haunted!"

"Why do you say that?" asked Professor Carver.

"Because . . . because . . ." She was trembling. She put her hands over her face.

"It's hard for her to talk about it," said Mr. Giddings. "She felt odd all the time we were there. Even when she was alone, she could feel eyes watching her. Once she saw something white go floating past the door. Isn't that right, dear?"

"Yes, yes!" she said, with her hands still over her face.

"I love Windy Hill," said Mr. Giddings, "but a man can't have his wife frightened out of her wits. We came back to Boston. Then I heard about you and I thought you might help me."

"How?" asked Professor Carver.

"I thought you might live in my house as you lived in the other one," said Mr. Giddings. "I thought you might drive out the ghost—if there is a ghost, of course."

"No, Mr. Giddings," said Professor Carver. "The whole idea is foolish."

Mrs. Giddings got to her feet. "You heard what he said. Now take me home!"

She and her husband went out together. She said, as they went down the stairs, "I *told* you we shouldn't have come here!"

Mr. Giddings

The next evening Jamie and Lorna were back in front of the candle shop. The air was still heavy and hot. They were still waiting for a breeze.

They heard the sound of carriage wheels.

"Maybe it's Mr. Giddings coming back," said Lorna.

"There's not much chance of that," said Jamie. "Father said no."

"I was sorry for Mr. Giddings," said Lorna.

"So was I," said Jamie.

"All those years he'd wanted that farm. Then, when he got it, he couldn't live there. I like the name Windy Hill," she said. "Shut your eyes, Jamie. Now think of Windy Hill and tell me what you see."

"I see a big house on a high hill," he said, "where the wind comes in from the sea."

"And it's night and there are trees all around,"

she said. "There's tall grass in the yard. An old man is creeping through the grass——"

"We'd better stop this game," said Jamie. "You'll be scaring yourself."

"No, I won't," she said.

"Remember the summer when Grandmother told us the stories about witches?" he said. "Afterward you walked in your sleep. Father said it was because you were upset."

"That was a long time ago. I wouldn't be upset now," said Lorna. "It's fun to pretend. Let's pretend some more about Windy Hill."

"Lorna, look," said Jamie.

The carriage had come into sight.

"Jamie, I was right!" she said.

The carriage stopped and Mr. Giddings got out. He was alone, except for the driver. "Good evening," he said. "Is your father at home?"

"Yes, sir," said Jamie.

"Would he see me again, do you think?" asked Mr. Giddings.

"I'll go ask," said Jamie.

He and Lorna ran upstairs.

"Mr. Giddings is here," said Jamie.

"He wants to see Father," said Lorna.

"What is it now?" asked Professor Carver. "Does he have another ghost story to tell us?"

"He looked so sad," said Mrs. Carver. "I wish you'd see what he wants."

"Oh, very well," said Professor Carver.

Jamie led Mr. Giddings up the stairs. They all sat in the little parlor.

"My wife didn't want me to come back," said Mr. Giddings, "but I felt I had to see you again. If you could help me——"

"How?" asked Professor Carver. "I can't drive a ghost out of a house when there's no ghost there."

"I know you don't believe in ghosts," said Mr. Giddings, "and you may be right. But if you went there and lived in the house——"

"Why?" asked Professor Carver.

"Because of my wife," said Mr. Giddings. "If she knows you lived there and saw no reason to be afraid, perhaps *she* wouldn't be afraid to go back. Don't you see?"

"Yes, I see," said Mrs. Carver.

"The farm is near Winton. You could drive out in less than a day," said Mr. Giddings. "All our things are in the house—chairs, tables, beds. You could move in tomorrow."

"We've never lived in the country," said Professor Carver. "We don't know how to run a farm."

"There'd be no work for you to do," said Mr. Giddings. "The handyman is there. He takes care of everything."

"It must be cooler in the country," said Mrs. Carver.

"Yes, indeed," said Mr. Giddings. "Windy Hill, we call it, because there's always a breeze."

Professor Carver said to his wife, "You want to go, don't you?"

"It's for you to say," she said.

He asked Jamie and Lorna, "Do you want to go?"

"It's for you to say," said Jamie.

"It must be pretty there," said Lorna.

Professor Carver said to Mr. Giddings, "I'd have to find someone to take my place at the school. Could you wait a week?"

"Certainly," said Mr. Giddings.

"And how long would you want us to stay?" asked Professor Carver.

"Do you think you might stay a month?" asked Mr. Giddings. "That would be till the end of summer."

Professor Carver looked at his wife. She nodded.

And Lorna whispered to Jamie, "We're going! We're going to Windy Hill!"

Windy Hill

They left Boston early one morning in Mr. Giddings' carriage. Mr. Giddings came with them. He rode inside with the Professor and Mrs. Carver. Jamie and Lorna rode outside on the driver's seat.

"This is the best place," said Jamie. "We can see the country."

They could talk with Riggs, the driver, too. He knew a story about every river they crossed and every town they passed.

They came to Winton.

Jamie and Lorna began to watch for Windy Hill.

"You can't quite see it from here," said Riggs. "I'll tell you when."

He took two pennies out of his pocket and held them in his hand. "I always like to have a little something for Bruno," he said.

"Who is Bruno?" asked Lorna.

"You'll soon be seeing him," said Riggs.

They came to the crossroads where bushes grew at the foot of a bank. A brown goat was tied to a bush. Nearby was a low cart with four wheels. Beside the cart sat a boy.

His hair was black and curly. His head was down so that his face was almost hidden. He sat in an odd way, with his legs doubled under him.

Riggs threw the pennies. They rolled in the dust by the road. The boy did not move.

The carriage went by. Jamie and Lorna looked back. They saw the boy's hands dart out and pick up the pennies.

"Now you've seen Bruno," said Riggs.

"Is he—is he a beggar?" asked Lorna.

"There's not much else he *can* be," said Riggs. "Bruno can't walk—hasn't walked since he was little, they tell me. Every morning he gets into that goat cart and comes rattling down to the crossroads. People go by, and nearly everybody gives him something."

"Does he have a father and mother?" asked Lorna.

"He has a father, but no mother that I know of," said Riggs. "They live off in the woods next to Windy Hill. See that stone fence? That's where Windy Hill begins."

"I see the house!" said Jamie.

It was a tall, square house set high on the hill ahead. A great tree spread its branches above the roof.

"There's a tower!" said Lorna.

"Old Jed Carey built the tower," said Riggs. "He lived there a hundred years ago. He kept thinking the Indians were coming to drive him out, so he put that tower on top of the house. Every day he'd go up there with his spyglass and keep watch. That went on for twenty years, but the Indians never came."

They were climbing the hill. The road was steep and rough.

Now Jamie and Lorna could see a small cottage near the big house.

"Who lives there?" asked Lorna.

"Stover, the handyman," said Riggs. "It's a wonder he's not out here to meet us."

They turned in at a driveway and stopped in front of the big house.

Mr. Giddings was the first one out of the carriage. "Welcome to Windy Hill," he said.

"It's beautiful," said Mrs. Carver.

"And wait till you see the rest—the woods and streams and fields," he said. "What do you think, Professor? Will you be able to paint pictures here?"

"I've seen a hundred things to paint already," said Professor Carver.

A man came out of the cottage. He was a small, bony-looking man, neither young nor old. Everything about him seemed faded, from his clothes to his hair to his pale blue eyes.

"Stover, this is Professor Carver," said Mr. Giddings, "and this is his wife and these are their children. They will be staying here for a while."

Stover blinked his eyes. "*Staying*, did you say, sir?"

"Yes," said Mr. Giddings. "Do what you can to make them comfortable. Their things are on top of the carriage. Help Riggs take them down."

He unlocked the front door. The Professor and Mrs. Carver followed him into the house. Jamie and Lorna walked behind them. They went down a hall and into a large parlor. Mr. Giddings raised the window shades. Sunlight shone in on the new chairs and tables, the rose-colored rug, the grandfather clock.

"The kitchen and pantry are on the other side," he said. "Here is a bedroom. You'll find more bedrooms upstairs."

"It's a lovely house," said Mrs. Carver.

"You'd never think it was haunted, would you?" said Mr. Giddings.

"I'm sure it isn't," she said.

"We'll see," said Mr. Giddings. "We should know by the end of summer, shouldn't we?"

"Windy Hill is not haunted. We can be sure of that already," said Professor Carver. "If something mysterious happens here, it still won't mean there's a ghost in the house. A strange sound might be the wind. A strange sight might be someone playing a joke."

"If something mysterious does happen while you're here, will you help me find out what it *really* is?" asked Mr. Giddings.

"Of course," said the Professor.

"Even if it means staying longer than a month?" asked Mr. Giddings.

"Yes, I'll help you, even if it means staying longer," said Professor Carver.

"Thank you," said Mr. Giddings. "You've made me feel better."

Within an hour he told them, "I must leave you now. My wife wants me back early. But I'll be stopping in again."

He said good-bye. As the carriage drove away, they could see his face in the window. He looked as if he were sorry to go.

The Tower

Mrs. Carver had brought food from the city. They were having supper in the kitchen when the handyman came to the door.

"Begging your pardon," he said, "there's milk and eggs in the springhouse. And there's garden stuff when you want it—corn and beans and onions—"

"Thank you, Stover," said Professor Carver.

"Where is the springhouse?" asked Mrs. Carver.

"Just down the walk there," said Stover.

"A springhouse!" said Mrs. Carver, after the handyman had gone. "We'll live like kings."

"What is a springhouse?" asked Lorna.

"Oh, you city children!" said Mrs. Carver. "You don't know about such things, do you? Come, let's see what we find."

They all went outside and down the walk. Behind the lilac bushes was a small stone house. Mrs. Carver opened the door. They could feel the coolness from inside. Water flowed across the stone floor about the pails and pans setting there.

"This little house was built over a spring," said Mrs. Carver. "We can keep milk and butter and eggs here. The cool water keeps them fresh."

"And see what's there in the orchard," said Professor Carver. "A beehive."

"Is there honey in it?" asked Lorna.

"We'll find out later," said the Professor. "We've had a full day and I think we're all a little tired. Shall we get ready for bed?"

"I want to choose my bedroom," said Jamie.

"I want to choose mine, too," said Lorna. "I've never had a room of my own."

"Why don't we all sleep in the same room tonight?" said Mrs. Carver. "By tomorrow we'll be used to the house and you can look at the other rooms."

They made beds in the big bedroom downstairs. Jamie made his bed on the floor by the window.

He lay there and looked out into the night. He was almost asleep when something moved close beside him.

He raised his head. At once he saw what had

moved. A breeze had blown the curtain out from the window.

He laughed to himself. But Mrs. Giddings would not have laughed, he thought. If she had seen the curtain move, she would have been sure a ghost was wandering through the house.

In the morning he and Lorna started upstairs. The steps were old and creaky.

"Every one makes a different sound." Lorna jumped from step to step. "You can almost play a tune on them."

Jamie had gone ahead and was looking down the upstairs hallway. "Six doors," he said. "That means six rooms up here."

"Six rooms!" said Lorna. "In the city we had only two altogether."

They went from one room to another, until they had seen them all.

"Which do you choose?" asked Lorna.

"The one at the head of the stairs," said Jamie. "I like the fireplace. If it gets cool enough before the end of summer, I'll build a fire."

Lorna chose the room just across the hall. "Because of the four-poster bed," she said.

"Let's go bring up our clothes," he said.

"Let's look at the attic first," said Lorna.

"I don't think there is an attic," he said.

"Then where does that go?" She pointed to the narrow stairway halfway down the hall.

"It probably goes to the tower." Jamie climbed the steps. They led through an opening in the ceiling. He went up through the opening and into the tower. He felt his way past a tiny window that let in only a little light. He could feel dust in his nose and cobwebs across his face.

At the top of the stairs was a square door. He pushed it open with his head. He stepped out onto the roof of the tower.

Lorna was close behind him. They stood together and looked over the wooden railing.

"We're almost in the middle of the big elm tree," she said. "We're like two birds in a nest."

"This tree couldn't have been here when old Jed Carey watched for Indians," said Jamie. "He wouldn't have seen far with all these leaves and branches in the way." He put his hand to his eye, as if he were looking through a spyglass. He said in a deep voice, "I am the ghost of old Jed Carey. Do you see any Indians down there?"

"Yes, they're all around us. Run for your life!" said Lorna.

She ran down out of the tower. He ran after her. The door fell shut with a crash.

They ran downstairs and through the parlor.

Mrs. Carver came out of the kitchen. "What on earth—?" she said.

"The Indians are coming!" said Lorna.

"It's a game," said Jamie.

He and Lorna ran out into the yard. They pretended to hide in the grass.

They rested there in the wind and sun.

"I like it here," said Lorna. "Don't you like it, Jamie?"

"Yes, I do," he said. "Of all the places we've lived, this is the best."

At the Crossroads

The next day they explored the woods.
"Could we get lost?" asked Lorna.

"We'll look for landmarks," said Jamie. "Then we can tell where we've been."

"This patch of strawberry plants can be a landmark," she said.

"And that birch tree, too," he said.

They walked through a bed of ferns. Jamie was ahead. "Be careful," he said. "Don't fall over this log."

There was no answer. He looked back. Lorna was standing still in the middle of the fern bed.

"What's the matter?" he asked.

"There's somebody spying on us," she said.

"Where?" he asked.

"Behind that tree," she said.

They stood looking at the tree.

25

"I thought I saw someone a while ago, but I wasn't sure," she said. "Now I *am* sure."

"Was it a man?" he asked.

"I couldn't tell," she said.

"Maybe it was a bird or a squirrel," he said.

"No. It was too big and too white." She stopped.

Very slowly someone was peeping out from behind the tree. First they saw a long, sharp nose, then the rest of the face. It was the face of an old, old woman.

She saw them watching her. Quickly she disappeared behind the tree. Then she peeped out again. The look in her eyes was both mischievous and shy.

She ducked her head. She seemed to be bowing to them.

Jamie bowed back. He said, "Good day, ma'am."

The old woman smiled. She said something in a singsong voice as she turned and hurried away. Leaves and flowers bobbed on her hat. In half a minute she was out of sight.

Lorna asked Jamie, "Could you tell what she said?"

He shook his head.

"I wonder why she was following us," said Lorna.

"If she's a spy, she doesn't know much about spying," said Jamie. "In that white dress and that hat she'd have a hard time hiding. And when we caught her, she didn't seem to care. It almost looked as if she *wanted* us to see her."

"Yes, it did," said Lorna. "It's a puzzle."

They walked on. Now and then they looked behind them, but they saw no more of the strange little woman.

They came to the road. Jamie helped Lorna over the fence and down the bank.

They took the road back toward the house. They came to the crossroads.

"There's Bruno," said Jamie.

The boy was sitting by the roadside where they had seen him the day before. The brown goat was tied to a bush nearby.

The boy's legs were doubled under him. His head was down.

"Good morning," said Jamie.

"Good morning, Bruno," said Lorna.

The boy did not answer.

Lorna whispered, "Maybe he can't talk."

The boy looked up. "I can talk when I want to," he said.

Lorna put out her hand and the goat came toward her. He gave her a friendly look out of his yellow-brown eyes. She touched his nose.

Bruno said sharply, "Leave him alone. He's mine."

"She was only going to pet him," said Jamie.

"I have some pennies," said Lorna. "If I'd known we were coming this way, I'd have brought them for you."

"I don't want your pennies!" shouted Bruno. "Go away and leave me alone!"

"But I didn't mean——" she began.

"Come on, Lorna," said Jamie, and they went away.

Lorna was troubled. "I shouldn't have said anything about the pennies. It was almost the same as calling him a beggar."

They walked up the hill. The sun was as warm as ever. Birds were singing in the trees. But some of the brightness had gone out of the morning.

The Man on the Bank

At supper that evening they talked about what had happened during the day.

"Stover went to town for me," said Mrs. Carver. "He brought back flour and sugar. Now I can cook."

"I set up a studio in the barn," said Professor Carver. "Now I can paint. I have so much room, I could open a school there."

Jamie and Lorna told about the little old woman in the woods.

"She may be a neighbor," said Mrs. Carver. "Perhaps she wondered who you were and what you were doing."

"We saw Bruno, too," said Jamie.

"And I'm sorry for what I said to him," said Lorna.

"What did you say?" asked her mother.

"I told him I wished I'd brought him some pennies," said Lorna.

"Isn't that why he sits there?" asked Professor Carver. "So people will give him money?"

"Yes," said Lorna, "but he doesn't want to talk about it."

"You didn't mean any harm," said Mrs. Carver. "Just watch your tongue after this and be as friendly as you can."

"I know something I could do," said Lorna. "I could make him some cookies. Do you think he would like that?"

"I should think so," said Mrs. Carver.

So the next day Lorna made cookies. As they baked in the oven, the smell of honey and spices filled the big kitchen.

It was afternoon before they were done.

"Why not take some to Bruno while they are still warm?" said Mrs. Carver.

Jamie and Lorna ran down to the crossroads. Bruno was sitting there with his eyes on the ground.

The goat tried to nibble at the paper bag in Lorna's hand.

"No, this is for Bruno," she said.

The boy spoke. "What's for Bruno?"

Lorna put the bag down in front of him.

"What's in it?" he asked.

"Look and see," she said.

"You're playing a joke on me," he said.

"No, we're not," she said.

"It's just an old empty sack. *I* know." But Bruno reached out and touched the bag. He looked inside it. "Cookies!" he said. He picked one up and dropped it back into the bag. "Where did you get them?"

"I made them," said Lorna.

"Ah—you can't make cookies," said Bruno.

"Yes I can," said Lorna, "and other things, too."

Bruno was frowning. "What did you bring me cookies for?"

"I thought you might like some," said Lorna.

"I—" He stopped. He was listening, as if he heard something they could not hear. He seized the bag of cookies and stuffed it inside his shirt. "Run!" he said.

"What—?" began Jamie. Then he and Lorna saw the man at the edge of the woods. He was a big man with a dark beard. Standing there on the bank, he looked like an angry giant. "Get out," he shouted, "and leave my boy alone!"

Jamie and Lorna stared at him.

"Get out," the man shouted again, "and don't you be coming back! D'you hear me? *Don't you be coming back!*"

Jamie caught Lorna's arm. They ran up the road.

Halfway up the hill they stopped for breath.

"He didn't have any right to talk to us that way," said Jamie. "He doesn't own the road."

"What was the matter with him?" she asked.

"I don't know," said Jamie. "Just because we were talking to Bruno—"

"Do you think he was Bruno's father?" asked Lorna.

"He must have been," said Jamie.

"Then I feel sorrier for Bruno than ever." She said after a while, "Isn't it odd, Jamie—?"

"What?" he asked.

"We came to Windy Hill because the house was supposed to be haunted," she said, "but it isn't haunted at all. It's the country around here that's strange!"

A Message from Bruno

In the morning Jamie and Lorna went out to find the handyman. They met him near the chicken house. He was carrying a basket of eggs.

"Mother is baking bread and we have to fill the woodbox," said Jamie. "Do you have a wheelbarrow we could use?"

"There's one in here. I don't use it very often." Stover went into a shed. He pushed aside an old spinning wheel and some jingling sleigh bells and dragged out a wheelbarrow.

Jamie thanked him. He started to push the wheelbarrow away.

But Stover wanted to talk. "I saw lights upstairs last night," he said.

"Jamie and I chose our rooms up there yesterday," Lorna told him.

"You don't say!" said Stover. "Do you sleep upstairs?"

"Yes," said Lorna.

"Aren't you afraid up there at night?" Stover gave them a sly look. "Don't you know about the ghost?"

"We've heard about it," said Jamie.

"But you don't believe in it?" asked Stover.

"Do you believe in it?" asked Jamie.

"Things happen hereabouts that would *almost* make you believe in ghosts," said Stover.

"What things?" asked Lorna.

"Well—just last month something happened," said Stover. "A man was coming through the woods. It was night and the moon was out. He saw something white in front of him, and he came running to tell me about the ghost he saw. He said it was wearing a hat and a white dress—"

Lorna broke in, "We were in the woods, and we saw someone wearing a hat and a white dress—"

"Ah, you've seen her, too," said Stover.

"Do you know her?" asked Lorna.

"I know her," said Stover. "That was Miss Miggie."

"Miss who?" asked Lorna.

"That's what she calls herself—Miss Miggie. Oh, she's a strange one." Stover shook his head.

"Lives in an old house on the next hill. Neat as a pin, they say, although I've never seen inside it. Sometimes she scares the daylights out of people, the way she wanders around day and night. Yet she wouldn't hurt a fly."

"Why does she wander around?" asked Lorna.

"You might say she's restless. She likes to keep moving," said Stover. "She likes to be close to people, too, and see what they're doing."

"She ran away from us," said Lorna.

"She's shy of strangers," said Stover. "Once she's used to you she'll stop and talk, as friendly as you please. Next time she comes by, you say to her, 'Good morning, Miss Miggie,' and see how pleased she'll be."

He started off with his basket of eggs. Jamie and Lorna walked with him as far as the house. Then they went on to the orchard.

Jamie pushed the wheelbarrow up to a stump that was old and falling apart.

"Mr. Giddings told us to take any dead wood we could find," he said. "Let's start with this."

They kicked and pulled at the stump until it fell to pieces. They began loading the wood into the wheelbarrow. While they were working, Lorna said in a low voice, "Jamie, she's here."

He looked up. Only a few steps away stood Miss Miggie. She was wearing her long dress and wide hat. Today there were grape leaves on her hat.

She spoke in a shy, chirping voice. "Happy day to you! Happy day!"

"Good day, Miss Miggie," said Jamie and Lorna.

"Do you know Bruno?" she asked. "Bruno-down-the-road?"

"Yes, we know him," said Lorna.

"I have a message. This is the message. Bruno —is—waiting." Miss Miggie ducked her head and backed away through the trees.

Lorna called to her, but the little old woman was already gone.

"How can she disappear so fast!" said Lorna. "What was it she said? 'Bruno is waiting.' What did she mean by that?"

"Perhaps he's waiting to see us," said Jamie. "Perhaps he sent Miss Miggie to tell us."

"We're not going, are we?" said Lorna.

"Why not?" he asked.

"You know what happened the last time," she said.

"If his father is there, we can go on by," said Jamie. "Or I'll go by myself if you'd rather."

"No, I'll go with you," she said.

They went down the hill to the crossroads. Bruno was there in his old place.

"We just saw Miss Miggie," said Jamie.

"Did you give her a message?" asked Lorna. "Did you want to see us?"

Bruno looked at them. He looked away.

Jamie and Lorna waited for him to speak.

He said at last, "I ate the cookies."

"Oh," said Lorna. "If you liked them, I'll bring you some more."

"But we don't want to make trouble for you," said Jamie.

"Trouble?" said Bruno.

"Your father didn't want us here yesterday," said Jamie.

Bruno said, "He doesn't want me—talking to people. But he sleeps all morning. In the morning—he—never—comes out."

Jamie pulled some tender weeds and fed them to the goat. Lorna sat down by the roadside. She picked three long blades of grass and began to braid them together.

"What's that?" asked Bruno.

"It's braiding," she told him.

He watched her hands. "I see how," he said.

He picked three blades of grass and began to braid them. His fingers were quick and strong.

"You can do it better than I can," said Lorna.

Jamie pulled more weeds and left them for the goat. He said to Lorna, "We left our load of wood in the orchard. Mother is waiting for it."

Lorna said to Bruno, "We have to go now."

"Are you coming back?" he asked.

"Yes, if you want us to," she said.

"You could come any morning," he said. "It's all right to come in the morning."

"We'll see," said Jamie, and he and Lorna said good-bye.

She asked on the way up the hill, "Why did he want to see us?"

"It may be," said Jamie, "that he wanted to thank us for the cookies."

"But he didn't thank us," she said.

"Perhaps he didn't know how," said Jamie. "You can tell he isn't used to talking to people very much."

"I can see why he wouldn't talk much at home." She asked, "Why do you suppose his father sleeps in the morning?"

Jamie shook his head.

"And why doesn't his father want him to talk to anyone?"

"There are too many mysteries here," he said. "Father would tell us not to worry our heads over them."

"We will go back to see Bruno, won't we?" she asked.

"Yes, we'll go back," he said.

"But just in the morning," said Lorna, "when that man is sure not to be there. I don't ever want to meet *him* again!"

Miss Miggie

A week passed, and Mr. Giddings drove out from Boston. He asked at once, "Has everything gone well? Have you seen anything strange?"

Professor Carver laughed. "No, not even one small ghost."

Mr. Giddings did not laugh. "I hope and pray you can say the same by the end of summer," he said.

He walked about the farm. Jamie and Lorna heard him talking to the chickens and pigs and cows. He started off into the woods. "Would you like to come along?" he asked, and Jamie and Lorna went with him.

"I played here when I was a boy," he told them. "Of course, these woods weren't mine then, but they were free to all. I knew every rock and tree."

They came to the stone fence that marked the

end of his land. On the other side was a house almost hidden by trees.

"The beggar boy lives there," said Mr. Giddings.

Jamie and Lorna climbed up on the fence where they could see the house better.

"It isn't very big," she said.

"The roof is falling in," said Jamie.

"Yes, and Tench will never fix it," said Mr. Giddings.

"Tench? Is he Bruno's father?" asked Lorna.

Mr. Giddings nodded. "And an ugly man he is."

"We know," said Lorna.

"He used to be my handyman," said Mr. Giddings, "but he was bad tempered, and lazy besides. One day I told him to leave my farm and never come back. After that he went from bad to worse. Now he goes to town every night and sits in the tavern. Then he sleeps half the next day."

"So that's why he doesn't come out in the morning," said Jamie.

"It makes a hard life for Bruno," said Lorna.

"You're bound to feel sorry for the boy," said Mr. Giddings, "though I hear he is just as bad tempered as his father."

"He may seem that way, but he really isn't," said Jamie.

"He's different than he was at first," said Lorna. "We go to see him every day."

"That's kind of you, I'm sure," said Mr. Giddings. "The boy needs friends. Sometimes Miss Miggie tries to look after him. But she's such a scatterbrain she can't look after herself."

They walked back to the house.

Mrs. Carver said, "Stay to supper, Mr. Giddings."

"Thank you kindly," he said, "but I told my wife I'd be back early."

Mrs. Carver said, "The next time you come, I hope she will be with you."

"The next time she comes," he said, "I hope it will be to stay."

After he had gone, Mrs. Carver said, "I wish he had stayed to supper. I'd have baked a pound cake."

"Couldn't you still bake one?" asked Jamie.

"I could," she said, "if I had wood in the woodbox."

Jamie and Lorna ran out to the garden where Stover was working.

"May we borrow your wheelbarrow?" asked Jamie.

Stover went to the shed. He said, as he brought out the wheelbarrow, "Ah, she's here already."

"Who?" asked Lorna.

Then they saw Miss Miggie standing in the shadow of the chicken house.

"She's come to hear the news," said Stover.

"What news is there?" asked Lorna.

"She knows Mr. Giddings was here," said Stover. "As soon as you're gone, she's going to ask me what happened."

"Why?" asked Lorna.

"She's curious, that's why. She's curious as a cat," said Stover. "She likes to find out things, and then she likes to tell them. She tells Bruno and the neighbors on the north and the neighbors on the south."

"But nothing happened," said Lorna. "Mr. Giddings just wanted to find out if we'd seen a ghost. And if there isn't a ghost by the end of summer, he and his wife will come to live here again."

"What will you do then?" asked Stover.

"Go back to Boston," said Jamie.

He and Lorna started off with the wheelbarrow.

"Shall we speak to Miss Miggie?" asked Lorna.

"She might not want us to," said Jamie. "She's almost hiding."

"I'm going to wave, anyway," said Lorna, and she waved her hand.

Miss Miggie stood still for a moment. Then she waved back and said in her thin, high voice, "Happy day!"

The Rag Bag

One morning Jamie and Lorna went down the road to see Bruno.

"This is for you," said Lorna, and she gave him a gingerbread boy.

Bruno ate it slowly. He asked her, "Did you make it?"

"Mother made it," she said.

"Did she know you brought it to me?" he asked.

"Yes," said Lorna.

"And she didn't care?"

"She *wanted* you to have it," said Lorna.

"She must be—a good lady," he said.

"She is a good lady and Father is a good man," said Lorna. "Wouldn't you like to see them? You could drive up some day."

"No," he said. "I couldn't do that."

They heard a wagon coming. Jamie and Lorna

went away into the woods. They knew that Bruno never liked anyone to see him pick up the coins people threw.

The wagon went by. They came out of the woods and sat down beside Bruno.

"What shall we talk about today?" asked Jamie.

"Tell about what you did in Boston," said Bruno.

"Well—we went to school," said Jamie.

"Did you walk or ride?" asked Bruno.

"We walked," said Lorna.

"What did you see on the way?" he asked.

"Mostly houses and churches and stores," she said.

"I'd like to go inside them," said Bruno. "Did you go inside?"

"Sometimes," said Lorna. "We went to church, and we went into the stores."

"Once we went to the theater," said Jamie.

"What was in the theater?" asked Bruno.

"There was a play," said Lorna. "Afterward people came out and sang and danced."

"And you came home and pretended you were the lady in the show," said Jamie. "She was funny, Bruno. She dressed up and danced and sang."

"Do it now!" said Bruno.

"That was a long time ago," said Lorna. "I don't remember the song."

"Do you know any songs?" asked Bruno.

"Oh, yes," said Lorna.

"Sing one," he said.

She sang a song about a pirate ship and a pirate crew.

When she finished, Bruno's eyes were bright. "Now I know it," he said. He began to sing in a strong, clear voice. He sang the song through to the end.

"You *do* know it," said Lorna.

"I learn every song I can," he said.

"I'll teach you another one," said Lorna.

"But not today," said Jamie. "It's time for us to go."

Bruno looked disappointed.

"I'll have time to teach you more songs," said Lorna. "We'll be at Windy Hill nearly another week."

"Another—week?" he said.

"Yes," she said, "because we——"

"Come on, Lorna," said Jamie.

He said, on the way up the hill, "It's getting to be afternoon. I was afraid Bruno's father might be up and walking this way."

"We don't want to make trouble for Bruno," said Lorna. "Jamie, did you hear the way he sang that song? And he'd heard it only once."

"He learns fast," said Jamie. "Think what he could learn in school."

"I don't suppose he's ever been to school," said Lorna.

"He must sit there by the road, winter and summer," said Jamie.

"I keep wishing we could do something to help him," said Lorna.

"There isn't much we can do," said Jamie, "except go to see him every day."

"And we can't do that much longer," said Lorna.

They came to the house. Mrs. Carver met them on the porch. She told Lorna, "A friend of yours was here."

"A friend of *mine?*" said Lorna.

"Miss Miggie. She left this with Stover and told him to give it to you." Mrs. Carver held up a flour sack tied with a ribbon.

Lorna opened the sack. It was filled with scraps of cloth.

"What shall I do with them?" she asked.

Mrs. Carver took out some of the pieces of cloth. Most of them looked new. "You could sew them into a quilt. That may be what Miss Miggie meant for you to do."

"I wonder why she gave me a present," said Lorna.

"She told Stover she liked you because you had such a friendly face," said Mrs. Carver.

"She has a friendly face, too," said Lorna. "I'll make a quilt out of these pieces and every time I see it, I'll remember Miss Miggie."

The Crazy Quilt

That afternoon Lorna began her quilt. "It's going to be a crazy quilt," she said. "Every piece will be a different size and shape."

After supper she took her work up to her room. She sewed in a piece of cloth, then another and another. After each one, she would say to herself—Just one more.

The house had grown quiet. She knew it must be long past bedtime. But she liked sitting there in the lamplight, in her own room, sewing on her quilt.

She began to nod. Her eyes closed. And suddenly she was wide awake. There was a sound of knocking in the room.

It was soft at first, then sharper and louder.

She looked out the open window into the night. The knocking stopped.

It was Jamie, she thought. He had knocked to let her know she should be in bed.

She went out into the hall. She tapped on Jamie's door.

After a few moments he asked in a sleepy voice, "What is it?"

"Did you knock?" she asked.

"Did I what?"

"Did you knock just now?"

"No," he said.

"I thought you did," she said, "but maybe . . . No, it wasn't anything."

She went back to her room. She went to bed and lay there, thinking. Had the sounds come from inside or outside? Or had she heard them at all? She might have gone to sleep in her chair. The knocking might have been part of a dream.

In the morning Jamie asked her, "What did you hear last night?"

"Nothing," she said. "It was just a dream."

After breakfast she and Jamie went to see Bruno for an hour. The rest of the day she worked on her quilt. Again she took it to her room after supper. She told herself, This time I won't sit up till I go to sleep and start dreaming.

It was early when she put her work aside. She was pleased with what she had done. It looked like a little quilt already.

She hung it on the chair before she went to bed.

She woke with the sun shining on her face. A robin was singing in the tree outside the window. She sat up and reached for her quilt.

She looked at the chair. She rubbed her eyes and looked again. The quilt was gone.

She got up and dressed. Out in the hall she met Jamie.

"Give it back," she said.

He stared at her.

"Give me my quilt," she said.

"I don't have your quilt," he said.

"You don't?"

"No, I don't."

"Cross your heart?"

"Cross my heart."

"I thought you took it—for a joke," she said.

"Well, I didn't," he said. "When did you have it last?"

"Last night," she said.

He went with her to her room. They looked together, behind the chair, under the table, under the bed.

"You see," said Lorna.

"You're right," he said. "It isn't here."

The Room
down the Hall

They went to breakfast. Mrs. Carver looked at their faces. "Is something wrong?" she asked.

"My quilt——" began Lorna.

"Are you having trouble?" asked Mrs. Carver. "I'll help you with it."

"My quilt is gone," said Lorna.

"How could it be gone?" asked Mrs. Carver.

"It was on my chair last night," said Lorna, "and now—"

Professor Carver asked Jamie, "Are you playing a joke on your sister?"

"That's what I thought," said Lorna, "but he isn't."

"Don't fret. We'll find it," said Mrs. Carver. "Quilts don't fly away."

After breakfast they all went upstairs. They looked in Lorna's room.

"It just isn't here," said Lorna.

"Have you looked anywhere else?" asked Professor Carver.

"It couldn't be anywhere else," she said.

"You haven't been using any of the other rooms?" asked Professor Carver.

"No," said Lorna.

They went out into the hall.

"That far door is open," said Professor Carver.

Jamie went down the hall and looked into the room. He went inside. He came out with something in his hand.

"My quilt!" said Lorna.

"It was on the floor," said Jamie. "Is it all right?"

She took the quilt. "Yes, it's all right. But how——?"

"You must have left it there," said Mrs. Carver.

"Mother, I didn't," said Lorna. "I haven't been in that room all week."

"You're sure?" asked Mrs. Carver.

"Of course I'm sure," said Lorna.

Mrs. Carver and the Professor looked at each other.

Mrs. Carver said, "Lorna, do you remember something that happened a long time ago? You were just a little girl, and one night we found you out of bed. You were opening the front door. Do you remember?"

"Yes," said Lorna. "I walked in my sleep."

"It may have happened again," said Mrs. Carver.

"Anyway, you have your quilt," said Professor Carver.

"Don't worry about it any more," said Mrs. Carver.

She and Professor Carver went downstairs.

Lorna walked slowly back into her room. Jamie went with her. She spread the quilt across the chair, where she had left it the night before.

"Do you think I walked in my sleep?" she asked.

"It could have happened," he said.

"And you think I took my quilt into that room and left it on the floor?" she asked.

"How else did it get there?" he asked.

"I don't know," she said, "unless somebody else was in the house."

"How could anybody come up those creaky stairs without waking us all up?" he asked. "And who would come in just to take your quilt off a chair and leave it in another room?"

She said nothing. She had no answer.

Late that morning they went to see Bruno.

"Are you going to teach me a song today?" he asked.

"I don't feel much like singing," said Lorna.

"Why not?" asked Bruno.

"Something happened last night," she said, "and I keep thinking about it."

"What happened?"

She told him about her quilt. "It was on that chair when I went to sleep. This morning it was gone."

Bruno looked from one to the other. "The ghost——" he said.

"There aren't any ghosts, Bruno," said Lorna. "I know what happened. I walked in my sleep."

"You *walked* in your *sleep?*"

"She took her quilt into another room," said Jamie, "and never even knew it."

"She did?" said Bruno.

Lorna tried to laugh. "You're looking at me as if *I'm* a ghost."

"Walking in your sleep," said Bruno. "I didn't know there could be such a thing."

"It happened to her once before," said Jamie.

"And I hope it never happens again," said Lorna.

The Sound of Bells

In the afternoon Lorna took her quilt to the orchard and worked on it there. Jamie came out and sat on the grass beside her.

"This is crooked and that is crooked!" Lorna put down her work. "Yesterday it was easy to do. Now I can't sew anything straight."

"Are you still worrying about last night?" he asked.

"I can't help it," she said. "How do people walk in their sleep? How do they see where they're going?"

"Their eyes are open," he said.

"In their *sleep?*"

"Yes," he said.

She made a face. "I don't like it. I don't want to get up in the dark and hide things from myself. If I walk in my sleep again, will you stop me?"

63

"I will if I hear you," he said.

"You'll hear me if I go downstairs," she said. "The steps will creak."

"But if you just walk down the hall, I might not hear you," he said. "I didn't last night."

"We could tie a string from my doorknob to yours," she said.

"Or we could set pots and pans outside your door—something that would make a noise," said Jamie. "I know what. The bells."

"What bells?" she asked.

"The sleigh bells in the shed where Stover keeps the wheelbarrow," said Jamie. "We could put them in front of your door."

"Yes!" she said. "And if I take a step outside, I'll be in the middle of them."

They went to the shed and brought out the bells. They were set in a row on a long leather strap.

"Stover went to town," said Lorna. "Shall we borrow them without asking him?"

"He won't mind," said Jamie. "We can tell him when he comes home."

He carried the bells into the house. He put them down in the hall in front of Lorna's door.

"There," he said. "If you take even one step outside, I'll hear you."

He lay awake that night. He saw the light come on in the cottage, and he knew that Stover had come back from town. He heard his father and mother walking about below. It was late before he went to sleep.

Suddenly he was awake again. The bells were ringing!

In a moment he was out of bed. He threw open the door. Stars were shining through the window at the end of the hall. By their light he could see a figure moving away from him.

"Lorna," he said.

The figure moved faster. It seemed to rise into the air. Then he saw that it was on the tower stairs.

"Lorna!" This time he shouted. He felt his way up the stairs. He reached for the figure ahead of him. He caught a handful of cloth.

Something struck him across the face. He was falling. The figure was falling with him. They landed together at the foot of the stairs.

He heard running steps. Then there was stillness.

He sat up. The bells were ringing again. Someone was coming toward him. He heard Lorna's frightened voice saying, "Jamie! Jamie!"

He got to his feet.

"Jamie, is it you?" she asked.

"Yes," he said.

Voices came from below. Professor Carver and Mrs. Carver came running up the stairs. The Professor was lighting the way with a candle.

"What are you doing up here?" he asked.

"I—I fell down the stairs," said Jamie.

"But we just came up the stairs," said the Professor.

"No, the *tower* stairs," said Jamie. "I thought Lorna was walking in her sleep. I wanted to stop her—before she got to the roof."

"I was in bed," said Lorna. "The bells woke me up."

They drew close together, a strange little group in their night clothes. Their faces were pale in the candlelight.

"Are you all right, Jamie?" asked the Professor.

"Yes," said Jamie.

Mrs. Carver had picked something up off the floor. "What is this?"

"It's a piece of grapevine," said the Professor.

"Here is another one," said Lorna.

"Who brought them in here?" asked the Professor.

"I never saw them before," said Jamie.

"Was somebody on the tower stairs?" asked Professor Carver.

"I told you—I thought it was Lorna," said Jamie. "There was *someone* up there. We fell down together, and I heard somebody run away."

"Back up the tower stairs?" asked Professor Carver.

"No," said Jamie.

"Nobody came downstairs," said Mrs. Carver, "because we were coming up."

"Then," said Professor Carver, "whoever it was is still here."

They looked down the hall. The far door was open.

With the candle in his hand, Professor Carver went to the door. "Who's there?" he called.

He went into the room. Jamie was close behind.

"The windows are locked," said Professor Carver. "No one could have got out that way."

Jamie pointed to the closet door. "Shall I look in here?"

"Stand back," said Professor Carver. "I'll look."

He opened the door. The light fell on someone standing very still in a corner of the closet. It was Bruno.

A Strange Story

Come out," said Professor Carver.

Bruno was trembling.

"Don't be afraid," said the Professor.

Bruno came out of the closet. He was walking, setting one bare foot in front of the other.

He put his hand to his arm. His teeth shut together as if he were in pain.

"Are you hurt?" asked the Professor.

"My arm," whispered Bruno. "When I fell down——"

Professor Carver felt the arm. "Don't try to move it," he said. "It may be broken."

There was a bed in the room. The Professor said, "Lie down here." He told Jamie, "Run over to the handyman's. Tell him we need a doctor."

Jamie hurried off. When he came back, Bruno was lying on the bed.

"Stover is going to town for the doctor," said Jamie.

Bruno was shivering, although the night was warm.

"He's having a chill," said Mrs. Carver, and she covered him with some of the bedclothes.

"What is Bruno doing here?" asked Lorna. "Why is he walking? I don't understand it."

"Neither do I," said the Professor. He asked Bruno, "Are you able to talk now? Do you know Mr. Giddings and his wife?"

"I used to see them," said Bruno.

"She thought there was a ghost in the house," said the Professor. "Were you the ghost?"

"No," said Bruno. "I never came in while they were here."

"When did you start coming in?" asked the Professor.

"After they went away, I came in," said Bruno. "I came in once—just to see the rooms. I didn't hurt anything."

"When was the next time you came in?" asked the Professor.

"Last night," said Bruno.

"What did you do last night?" asked the Professor.

"I—I took the sewing off the chair in Lorna's room," said Bruno.

"You took my quilt?" said Lorna. "Then I *didn't* walk in my sleep."

"And I—I knocked on your window the night before," said Bruno. "I was in the tree—where I could see—and I took a long stick and——"

"How could you do that?" asked Lorna. "We were your friends."

Bruno's eyes filled with tears.

Mrs. Carver sat down by the bed. "Why don't you tell us why you did it?" she asked.

"I wanted Jamie and Lorna to stay," he said.

Mrs. Carver said, "I don't know what you mean."

"Miss Miggie told me you were here looking for a ghost," said Bruno. "Then she said if you didn't find one by the end of summer you were going away. So I tried to do things to—to make you think there *was* a ghost. But nobody said anything after I knocked on the window. When I took the sewing out of Lorna's room, nobody thought it was a ghost. So tonight I came in——"

"How?" asked Professor Carver.

"Through the tower. I climbed the big tree and got on top of the tower, the way I did before. I lifted up the door——"

"What were you going to do tonight?" asked Professor Carver.

"Well—I had some pieces of vine. I was going

to leave one on Jamie's door and one on Lorna's so they'd *see* something had been in the house. I was going to knock and run away before anyone had time to catch me. But I stepped on some bells, and Jamie came after me. He caught me and I fell down, and then I ran in here——"

Jamie and Lorna were close to the bed, listening. Jamie said, "You did all that just because you wanted us to stay?"

"There never was anyone before—anyone to come and see me—and talk to me every day," said Bruno. "I didn't do it to make you afraid. I just didn't want you to go away. And Miss Miggie said when you went away, you'd never come back."

"You climbed that tree and got in through the tower," said Lorna, "and all the time we thought you couldn't walk."

"I—I didn't——" he began.

"You don't have to say any more now," said Mrs. Carver. "Rest a while."

"No, I'll tell you," he said.

The story he told was long and strange. Sometimes he closed his eyes, as if he were ashamed.

He could not remember his mother and father, he said. When he was small, he lived with his Aunt Rosa. One day he ran into the street and was struck by a coal wagon. Afterward he could not walk.

His aunt was often ill. At last she had to go away to a hospital, and he was left in a home for orphans.

A man came to see the orphans. He said he wanted to give Bruno a home. The man was Tench. He took Bruno away.

They went to New York City. Tench taught the boy to beg on the street. Many people would give money to a boy who could not walk.

Bruno gave Tench the money. Tench gave him food and clothing and a place to sleep.

As Bruno grew older, he grew stronger. Every day he tried to walk. This made Tench angry. But whenever Bruno was alone, he kept trying to stand and walk.

They had to leave the city. Tench was in trouble with the police, although Bruno did not know why. They came to the country. Tench set the boy to begging at the crossroads near Windy Hill.

By this time, Bruno could walk. At night, when Tench went to the tavern, Bruno walked about the house. He went outside. Soon he was running and jumping and climbing.

But every day he dragged himself into the goat

cart and let Billy pull him down to the crossroads. It was what Tench wanted him to do.

Once Tench saw him walking and beat him
with a stick. He said, "Don't ever let anyone see
you walk. If you do, you'll never get another
penny without working for it. And if you
worked, you wouldn't make half as much as people give you now."

Bruno thought of running away. Tench
seemed to know what he was thinking. "You
can't get away," he said. "There's no place where
you can hide from me."

And Bruno was afraid.

The doctor came and looked at Bruno's arm.
"No bones broken," he said, "but it's a bad
sprain." He tied the arm up in a bandage and
sling. "Get a good night's rest, and I'll be back
to see you in a day or two."

Mrs. Carver said, after the doctor had gone,
"Let's all try to get a good night's rest. This will
be your bed, Bruno."

He looked frightened. "I can't stay here. I
have to get back, before he finds out——"

"If you went back with the bandage on your
arm, you'd have to tell him," said Jamie. "It's
better to stay here."

"You'd let me stay, after what I did?" asked Bruno.

"We know now why you did it," said Jamie.

Lorna looked at her father. "He doesn't have to go back, does he?"

"No," said the Professor. "He doesn't ever have to go back."

The End of Summer

In the morning Professor Carver came upstairs to look at Bruno. Mrs. Carver and Lorna were sitting by his bed.

"He's asleep and quiet now," said Mrs. Carver.

"Once he was having a bad dream," said Lorna.

"I should think most of his life has been a bad dream," said Professor Carver. "It's hard to believe there are people in the world like Tench."

Jamie had come to the door. Professor Carver asked him, "Do you know where the man lives?"

"Yes," said Jamie.

"Take me there," said Professor Carver.

Jamie led the way to Tench's house. They had to walk through a tangle of weeds to get to the door.

Professor Carver knocked. He knocked again. Then they saw Tench at the window, watching them. His hair was matted. His eyes were red.

"I want to talk to you about Bruno," said Professor Carver.

"Bruno? You know where he is?" Tench said in a hoarse voice, "You get him back here!"

"He isn't coming back," said the Professor.

Tench began to shout. His words ran together.

"Listen to me," said Professor Carver. "We know the boy is not your son. We know enough about you to —"

Tench shouted something else, but now there was fear in his voice. He slammed the window shut.

"Very well," Professor Carver called after him, "but you'll hear more of this."

He and Jamie walked back through the woods. The morning was still. A mist hung over the trees.

"In all the excitement, I'd forgotten what day it is," said Professor Carver. "Do you remember?"

Jamie shook his head.

"It's the last day of summer," said Professor Carver. "We've been here a month today."

"It doesn't seem that long," said Jamie. "I wish we were staying longer."

"So do I," said Professor Carver, "although I didn't much want to come at first. Some good things have happened since we've been here. We've taken Bruno away from Tench. That's the best thing."

"Is Bruno going to stay with us?" asked Jamie.

"Yes, until we can be sure where he belongs," said Professor Carver. "I hope we can find some of his people."

"What if we can't?" asked Jamie.

"Then perhaps he belongs with us," said Professor Carver. "Jamie, there's something else good that we've done by coming here. We stayed till the end of summer without seeing a ghost. Now I think Mr. Giddings and his wife can be sure there's no ghost at Windy Hill."

"When are they coming back?" asked Jamie.

"I expect them today, if Mr. Giddings hasn't forgotten," said the Professor.

"And we'll go back to Boston?" asked Jamie.

"Yes," said the Professor. "Back to our rooms over the candle shop—unless someone has another haunted house for us to live in!"

Mr. Giddings had not forgotten. Early in the

afternoon his carriage drove up, and he and his wife got out. She looked pale and almost ill, but Mr. Giddings was beaming.

They all sat on the porch. Bruno sat on the steps between Jamie and Lorna.

"Isn't that the beggar boy?" asked Mr. Giddings. "I always thought he was crippled."

"Not now," said Professor Carver, "but he fell and hurt his arm. We're looking after him."

"Very kind of you, I'm sure." Mr. Giddings leaned back in his chair. "Well, today is the day."

"Yes," said Professor Carver. "The last day of summer."

"And all this time you've been happy at Windy Hill?" asked Mr. Giddings.

"Most happy," said Professor Carver.

"Did you hear? Are you listening, dear?" Mr. Giddings asked his wife.

She bowed her head.

"Tell me this," said Mr. Giddings. "Since you came to the country, have you seen a ghost?"

"We have not," said Professor Carver.

"Have you heard a ghost?" asked Mr. Giddings. "Have you felt a ghost in the house with you?"

"Never," said Professor Carver.

"You heard what he said?" Mr. Giddings patted his wife's hand. "There's no ghost at Windy Hill. We can come back, my dear. We can come back!"

Mrs. Giddings looked out toward the road and the woods. She closed her eyes.

"Aren't you glad?" asked her husband.

"I—I—" She began to sob. "I can't stand it any more!"

"Can't stand what, my dear? What are you saying?"

"I have to tell you!"

"What's wrong?" he asked. "Tell me."

"You're so good. You've always been so good," said Mrs. Giddings, "and I'm so wicked."

"No, no," said Mr. Giddings.

"Yes, I am." Mrs. Giddings was still sobbing. "There never was a ghost here. I knew it all the time."

"But you told me——" he said.

"That woman—Miss Miggie—went past the door one day. She frightened me, until I saw who she was," said Mrs. Giddings. "But I saw how easy it would be to pretend I'd seen a ghost. So I pretended——"

"But *why?*" asked her husband.

"Because I couldn't bear to live here," she

said. "It's so far out in the country—so far from my mother and all my friends. You loved it so, I didn't know how to tell you. That's why I pretended there was a ghost. Today you were so happy to be coming back, I thought I'd try to be happy here, too. But I can't—I can't!"

She ran down the porch steps and threw herself into the carriage.

Mr. Giddings ran after her. He climbed into the carriage and sat beside her.

Soon he called the driver.

Riggs came out of the handyman's house. He untied the horses and turned the carriage about.

Mr. Giddings came back to the house. "I don't know what to say—I really don't," he said. "Poor little woman, she's so upset. I had no idea how she felt. Of course she doesn't have to live here. I can buy her the finest house in Boston." He said to Professor Carver, "Would you stay on here for a while, till I can get my wits together?"

"Of course we'll stay," said the Professor.

"Thank you kindly." Mr. Giddings left them. The carriage rolled out of the driveway and down the hill.

Professor Carver said, "Of all the strange things I've ever heard——"

"I'm sorry for him," said Mrs. Carver. "He does love this farm. Now he has to live in the city."

"Mr. Giddings will be happier there," said the Professor, "as long as she is happy."

On the step, Jamie, Lorna, and Bruno had been talking, with their heads close together. Jamie said to his father, "Bruno is worried about Billy."

"Billy?" asked the Professor.

"His goat," said Jamie. "He is afraid Billy will be hungry. Tench never takes care of him."

"I'll go look after him," said the Professor.

Jamie went with his father. When they looked back, Lorna and Bruno were following.

"Come along," said the Professor, "but Bruno had better keep out of sight."

They came to the stone fence. Lorna and Bruno waited there. Professor Carver and Jamie went up to the house.

The door was open.

"Tench!" called the Professor.

He looked in. There was only one room in the house. It was empty, with clothing and papers thrown about, as if someone had left in a great hurry.

"I think we've seen the last of Tench," said the Professor.

Jamie was looking behind the house. The goat was there in his pen.

"Come, Billy." Jamie found a rope on the gate. He tied it to Billy's halter and led the goat out of the pen.

When they came to the stone fence, Jamie and the Professor lifted Billy over.

Bruno put an arm about the goat's neck. Billy nibbled at the buttons on Bruno's shirt.

They walked through the woods.

Someone looked out from behind a tree ahead. It was Miss Miggie in her long, white dress with flowers on her hat.

"She knows something has happened," said Lorna. "She wants to hear the news."

Miss Miggie waved her hand. "Happy day!" she called.

"Happy day, Miss Miggie," said Jamie and Lorna, and Bruno said it too.

ABOUT THE AUTHOR

Clyde Robert Bulla was born near King City, Missouri. He received his early education in a one-room schoolhouse, where he began writing stories and songs. After several years as a writer of magazine stories, he finished his first book, then went to work on a newspaper.

He continued to write, and his books for children became so successful that he was able to satisfy his desire to travel through the United States, Mexico, Hawaii, and Europe. He now lives in Los Angeles.

In 1962, Mr. Bulla received the first award of the Southern California Council on Children's Literature for distinguished contributions to that field. He has written more than thirty stories for young readers.

ABOUT THE ARTIST

Don Bolognese was born in New York and was graduated from the Cooper Union school of art where he is an instructor. Mr. Bolognese is the illustrator of the Crowell Holiday Book *Washington's Birthday,* by Clyde Robert Bulla.

Don Bolognese and his family live in Brooklyn, New York. Their summer house in Vermont is similar to the setting for the house on "Windy Hill."

BY THE AUTHOR:

Benito

The Donkey Cart

Down the
  Mississippi

Eagle Feather

Flowerpot
  Gardens

The Ghost of
  Windy Hill*

Ghost Town
  Treasure*

Indian Hill

John Billington,
  Friend of
  Squanto

Johnny Hong of
  Chinatown

Jonah and the
  Great Fish

The Moon Singer

New Boy in
  Dublin

Old Charlie

Pirate's Promise

The Poppy Seeds

A Ranch for
  Danny

Riding the Pony
  Express

The Secret Valley

Song of St. Francis

Squanto, Friend of
  the Pilgrims*

Star of Wild Horse
  Canyon*

The Sugar Pear
  Tree

Surprise for a
  Cowboy

The Sword in the
  Tree

Three-Dollar Mule

Viking Adventure

White Bird

White Sails to
  China

*Paperback edition, Scholastic Inc.